S0-DVD-826

I LOVE YOU AND CHEESE PIZZA

I LOVE YOU AND CHEESE PIZZA copyright © by Summer and Muu, Brenda Li.

All rights reserved.

www.SummerandMuu.com

No portion of this book may be reproduced in any form, any manner whatsoever, stored in any retrieval system, or transmitted in any form by any means without permission from the publisher/author.

For permissions contact:

Brenda@SummerandMuu.com

This book is a work of fiction. Names, characters, places and incidents are either the product of the author's imagination or are used fictitiously, and any resemblance to actual persons, living or dead, business establishments, events or locales is entirely coincidental.

Paperback:

ISBN-13: 978-1-77447-008-4

ISBN-10: 1-77447-008-X

Published by Summer and Muu

Printed and Made in United States

Summer and Muu, Summer and Muu Kids and associated logos are trademarks and/or registered trademarks of Summer and Muu.

Dedicated to my two troublemakers,
Kobe and Chase.

Brian is a pig in jeans.
One day, he noticed
something new on the wall.

love

"Mom? What does this say?"
Brian asked.

"LOVE is a sweet feeling. When you see someone you reeeaally love, you feel happy. You care about them A LOT," Mom explained.

So, is there someone you reeeeally LOVE?
Hmmmm.....
Maybe it starts with the letter M?
HINT
HINT
love

"YA! **Mike** the pizza guy!"
Brian yelled.

I love it when he delivers my cheese pizza!

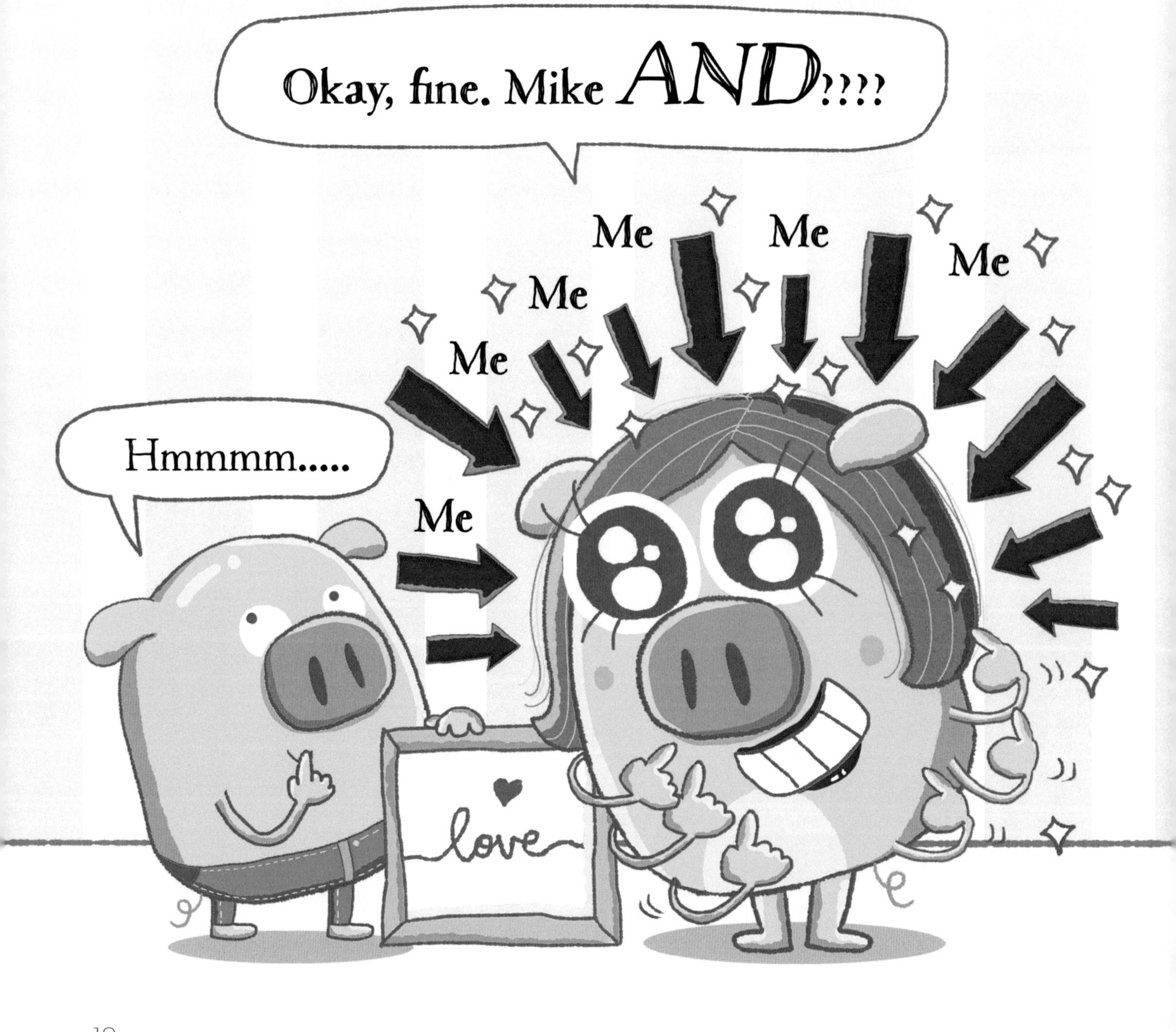
Okay, fine. Mike AND????
Hmmmm.....
Me
Me
Me
Me
Me
Me
love

"Love is also when you stand up for your little sister when she gets bullied at school."

"Love is when your teacher patiently explains a math question to you."

"Love is when you hug Grandma and Grandpa."

"Love is also when daddy throws you into the air."

Wheeee!!

"How can I show people I love them?"
Brian wanted to know.

Well, it can be as easy as just saying "I Love You". You can give them a hug. You can be kind and caring. You can even draw a card!

So Brian started drawing cards with hearts.

He gave cards to Grandma and Grandpa.

He gave a card to his sister.

A card to his friend.

A card to his teacher.

23

And a card to his dad.

WAIT!
There are more!

Brian carried a HUGE pile of cards down the stairs.

25

But his left foot tripped over his right foot...

OOU!

OW!

BONK!

BOING!

AIYEEEEE!

Brian bumped his head and crashed into the plant.

Mom ran over,
looking concerned.

"Sorry Mom, I broke your favorite plant," Brian apologized.

"Oh Brian, that's alright! As long as you are safe, nothing else matters. Are you okay?"

"No, Mom, these are ALL for you,"
Brian continued to explain.

"LOVE is when you rushed over when I fell."

"LOVE is when you forgave me when I broke your plant."

"LOVE is when you asked if I was okay."

"LOVE is when you show me the true meaning of love,

EVERY DAY!"

LET'S CHAT ABOUT LOVE!

1) What is love?

2) How does love make you feel?

3) Who are the people you love?

4) What are some ways that you can show people you care about them?

BONUS CHEESE MAZE!

Help Brian get to his cheese pizza!

Hope you enjoyed the book!
Please leave me a
review on Amazon!

FREE COLORING PRINTABLES:
SummerandMuu.com/freebie